My dearest pup

I hope this letter reaches you safe and sound. You have been so brave since you had to flee from the evil wolf Shadow.

Do not worry about me. I will hide here until you are strong enough to return and lead our pack. For now you must move on – you must hide from Shadow and his spies. If Shadow finds this letter I believe he will try to destroy it . . .

Find a good friend – someone to help finish my message to you. Because what I have to say to you is important. What I have to say is this: you must always

ely. Trust in your friends

Sue Bentley's books for children often include animals, fairies and wildlife. She lives in Northampton and enjoys reading, going to the cinema, relaxing by her garden pond and watching the birds feeding their babies on the lawn. At school she was always getting told off for daydreaming or staring out of the window – but she now realizes that she was storing up ideas for when she became a writer. She has met and owned many cats and dogs and each one has brought a special kind of magic to her life.

Sue Bentley

A Forest Charm

Illustrated by Angela Swan

PUFFIN

Charlie — cute funny-face, cat lover

PUFFIN BOOKS

Published by the Penguin Group
Penguin Books Ltd, 80 Strand, London WC2R 0RL, England
Penguin Group (USA) Inc., 375 Hudson Street, New York, New York 10014, USA
Penguin Group (Canada), 90 Eglinton Avenue East, Suite 700, Toronto, Ontario, Canada M4P 2Y3
(a division of Pearson Penguin Canada Inc.)
Penguin Ireland, 25 St Stephen's Green, Dublin 2, Ireland (a division of Penguin Books Ltd)
Penguin Group (Australia), 250 Camberwell Road, Camberwell, Victoria 3124, Australia
(a division of Pearson Australia Group Pty Ltd)
Penguin Books India Pvt Ltd, 11 Community Centre, Panchsheel Park, New Delhi – 110 017, India
Penguin Group (NZ), 67 Apollo Drive, Rosedale, North Shore 0632, New Zealand
(a division of Pearson New Zealand Ltd)
Penguin Books (South Africa) (Pty) Ltd, 24 Sturdee Avenue, Rosebank,
Johannesburg 2196, South Africa

Penguin Books Ltd, Registered Offices: 80 Strand, London WC2R 0RL, England

puffinbooks.com

First published 2008
010

Text copyright © Sue Bentley, 2008
Illustrations copyright © Angela Swan, 2008
All rights reserved

The moral right of the author and illustrator has been asserted

Set in Bembo
Typeset by Palimpsest Book Production Limited,
Grangemouth, Stirlingshire
Made and printed in England by Clays Ltd, St Ives plc

British Library Cataloguing in Publication Data
A CIP catalogue record for this book is available from the British Library

ISBN: 978-0-141-32380-0

www.greenpenguin.co.uk

MIX
Paper from
responsible sources
FSC
www.fsc.org
FSC® C018179

Penguin Books is committed to a sustainable
future for our business, our readers and our planet.
This book is made from Forest Stewardship
Council™ certified paper.

Prologue

The young silver-grey wolf padded
through the trees. Patches of snow still
lay on the hillside, gleaming in the
spring sunlight. Storm lifted his head.
It felt good to breathe the cold air of
his home.

Suddenly, a terrifying howl rang out.

'Shadow!' Storm gasped. The fierce
lone wolf who had attacked the

Moon-claw pack and wounded Storm's mother was very close.

There was a flash of bright golden light and a shower of dazzling sparks. Where the young wolf had been standing there now crouched a tiny puppy with fluffy white fur, a stocky body and short legs.

Storm whined with terror and his little puppy heart beat fast. He hoped this disguise would protect him from his enemy.

His puppy paws kicked up the soft snow as he tore through the trees. There was a steep ridge ahead of him. Perhaps there would be somewhere to hide. Storm glimpsed a tangle of tree roots that had formed a natural cave and headed towards them.

As he approached, Storm saw wolf eyes gleaming from within the darkness of the roots. He caught his breath and skidded to a halt, ready to turn and run away as fast as he could.

'Storm! In here, quickly!' the wolf called out in a soft growl.

'Mother,' Storm sighed with relief. He rushed forward and pushed through the tangled roots until he reached the she-wolf.

'It is good to see you again, my son,' Canista rumbled, licking her disguised cub's fluffy white fur and little square muzzle.

Storm yipped a greeting. He wriggled his body and wagged his stumpy tail as he licked his mother's face. 'I have come back to lead the Moon-claw pack!'

Canista's gentle eyes lit up with pride.
'Bravely said, but now is not the time.
Shadow wants to be leader and he is
too strong for you. He has already
killed your father and litter brothers and
left me weak from his poisoned bite.'

Storm curled his lip in a growl,
showing small sharp teeth. He knew
that his mother was right, but he was
reluctant to leave her.

'The other wolves will not follow
Shadow – they are waiting for you. Go
back to the other world. Use this
disguise. Return when you are stronger
and wiser, and then face Shadow.' As
Canista finished speaking, she gave a
wince of pain.

Storm huffed out a shimmering gold
puppy breath, which swirled around his

mother's wounded paw and then disappeared into her grey fur.

Canista narrowed her eyes. 'Thank you. The pain is easing.'

Another fierce howl rang out, sounding much closer.

'Shadow knows you are here. Go. Save yourself!' Canista urged.

Bright gold sparks bloomed in the tiny puppy's downy white fur. Storm whimpered as he felt the power building inside him. The gold light around him grew brighter. And brighter . . .

Chapter
ONE

Cassie Yorke stamped moodily through the forest in her new walking boots. She was with her mum and dad and about twenty other adults and kids.

'Why do we have to do this stupid family team-building thing anyway?' she complained.

Mrs Yorke gave her daughter a patient smile. 'That's the third time you've

asked me that since leaving home,
Cassie. Your dad's new boss is really
keen on encouraging his staff to get
along well with each other. And that
includes their families. This weekend is
a way of us working as a team and
getting to know each other better,' she
explained.

'But we're going to be camping. How

can that be a challenge?' Cassie asked.

'Ever tried camping without a tent to sleep in, a stove to cook on and no water on tap?' her dad asked.

'No way!' Cassie said, horrified.

Her mum laughed. 'We are meant to have fun too. Now try and lose the long face, Cass. OK?'

Cassie sighed heavily and felt her shoulders drooping to match her face. Traipsing through a cold muddy forest on a Friday afternoon was definitely *not* her idea of fun! She had been planning to curl up by the log fire in the sitting room and finish reading her book. *Lost in the Amazon* was the latest in the series about the amazing adventures of ace explorer Jilly Atkins.

Her dad came over and put his arm

round her shoulder. 'Come on, Cass. Where's your spirit of adventure? Just try and imagine you're Jilly Atkins!' he suggested cheerily.

'As if!' Cassie said.

Jilly was tall, strong and brave and fearless. Not small and rather dumpy, like Cassie felt, and she had probably never been teased for being a slowcoach when doing school sports.

'Here we are now,' Mrs Yorke said as the group came in sight of a large wooden cabin with a sign above the door that read *Wild Wood Experiences*.

After the welcome and introductions, two instructors divided the group into teams: the Reds, Blues and Greens. Cassie and her mum and dad were in the Reds.

'Oh great. We've been teamed up with Ronson from the office. He's a real know-it-all,' Mr Yorke said softly.

Cassie saw a fit-looking man who towered over her dad. Mr Ronson was tanned and broad-shouldered and

looked as if he practically lived at the gym. His wife and daughter were both slim and dark-haired.

'Well, we're supposed to be getting to know each other better. Shall we go over and say hello?' Cassie said.

Mr Yorke gave her a mournful look. Despite herself, Cassie couldn't help smiling.

As the adults exchanged greetings, Cassie went over to Mr Ronson's daughter. 'Hi, I'm Cassie.'

'I'm Erin,' the girl said, tossing her long silky hair over her shoulder.

Cassie looked at her enviously. She wished her hair would grow that long, but her blonde curls just seemed to grow outwards and get bushier.

Erin didn't really say much. Cassie

thought she might be shy, so she made a special attempt to be friendly. 'I'm dreading this. I've never been even normal camping or anything. Have you?' she asked, smiling.

Erin shrugged. 'No, but I've done loads of outdoor stuff with my dad. This is going to be easy-peasy. But how come *you're* here? The rules say you have to be at least ten before you can take part.'

'I'm almost eleven actually,' Cassie said, her smile wavering.

'But you're so small! I thought you were only about eight,' Erin said rudely, looking Cassie up and down.

'My gran says good things always come in small packages,' Cassie shot back. She was used to people making comments about her size and usually found that making a joke of it got over any awkwardness.

But Erin didn't even grin. 'Yeah, well, your gran would have to say that, wouldn't she? I just hope you're not going to hold our team back. My dad only plays to win. He always says that you don't get any prizes for coming second.'

Good for him, Cassie thought, starting to feel rattled. 'My dad's motto is "It's the taking part that counts". I like that one much better!'

'Huh!' Erin gave Cassie a pitying look before flouncing over to stand with her mum.

Mrs Yorke noticed her daughter's annoyed face. 'Are you OK, Cassie? You're not still sulking, are you?'

'Of course not. I'm fine now,' Cassie fibbed, pasting on her best fake smile.

After meeting Erin, Cassie wished more than ever that she could be at home with her head in her book. There didn't seem much chance of the two of them making friends this weekend.

Before the teams set off into the forest, the instructors gathered them all together again for a few words about health and safety. Cassie's tummy suddenly growled, making everyone laugh.

It had been a long drive to get there and lunch seemed like hours ago. Cassie felt more than ready for a snack. There were some crisps and chocolate in her rucksack, but she hesitated about getting them out. Erin was looking her way and she didn't fancy getting any more sarcastic comments.

As people stood about chatting outside the cabin, Cassie saw a chance to slip away. 'Just popping to the loo!' she called to her dad.

'OK, honey. Don't be long,' he said.

Cassie headed past the loo and nipped

smartly round the back of the cabin.
She was alone with just the open forest
in front of her. Fishing in her rucksack,
she drew out a bar of chocolate.

'Yum, yum,' Cassie breathed, licking
her lips.

She was about to take a big luxurious
bite, when suddenly, a dazzling bright
flash of gold light shot out in all
directions from the bush in front of her.

Cassie blinked hard, blinded for a
moment. She rubbed her eyes and saw
a tiny cute puppy with fuzzy white fur,
a stocky body and short legs crawling
out of the bush.

'Can you help me, please?' it woofed.

Chapter
TWO

Cassie gaped at the little white puppy in utter amazement and the chocolate bar slipped from her numb fingers on to the ground.

She must be so hungry that she was hearing things! Talking puppies didn't just appear to small rather ordinary girls. Even Jilly Atkins had never met one and she'd explored all kinds of strange and remote places.

Cassie shook her head, laughing at herself. Her dad always said that she had an over-active imagination.

'Hello, you,' she crooned, rubbing her fingers together to encourage the tiny puppy to come closer. 'I think you must be a little Westie. Aren't you gorgeous? I wonder which of the instructors you belong to.'

The puppy pricked its ears, and two bright midnight-blue eyes looked up at her from behind a little fringe of fluffy white fur. 'I belong to no one but myself. I am Storm of the Moon-claw pack.'

Cassie did a double take. She snatched her hand back as if it had been burned. 'Y-you really c-can talk?' she gasped.

'Yes, I can. Who are you?' the puppy yapped.

Cassie still couldn't quite believe this was happening, but she didn't want to scare the amazing puppy away. She squatted down to make herself seem smaller and less threatening.

The puppy pricked its ears and put its little head on one side, waiting for her to answer. Although Storm was really

tiny, he seemed quite sure of himself.

'I'm Cassie. Cassie Yorke. I'm here with my parents to do some family team building. It's part of Dad's new job,' she explained.

Storm bent his neck in a formal bow. 'I am honoured to meet you, Cassie.' He took a few steps closer and reached out his neck.

Cassie grinned delightedly as the cute puppy's button-like black nose twitched and then she felt the little wet tip brushing against her fingers. She gently rubbed Storm's soft chest and then moved up to stroke his ears.

It still felt really weird to be having a conversation with a puppy, but Cassie's curiosity began to take over from her initial shock. 'We're miles from anywhere in the middle of this forest. How come you're here if you don't belong to anyone?' she asked, puzzled.

Storm's tiny body began trembling all over like a leaf. 'An evil lone wolf called Shadow is looking for me. He killed my father and litter brothers and injured my mother. Shadow wants to lead the Moon-claw pack, but the others will not follow him while I live.'

'But you're just a helpless little puppy. Why would an evil wolf –' Cassie began.

Storm backed away. 'I will show you!'

There was another flash of bright gold light, and big sparks rained down all around Cassie and sizzled on the damp forest floor as they landed.

'Oh!' Cassie cried, blinking hard. But

as her sight cleared, she caught her breath.

The tiny white puppy had disappeared and in its place there crouched a majestic young silver-grey wolf with bright midnight-blue eyes. Specks of gold dust gleamed in its fur and shone from within its deep neck-ruff.

Cassie eyed the wolf's sharp teeth and

powerful muscles. 'Storm?' she breathed
nervously.

'Yes, it is me. Do not be afraid. I will
not harm you,' Storm told her in a
deep velvety growl.

While Cassie was still struggling to take
in the sight of Storm as his magnificent
real self, there was a final dazzling flash
and Storm reappeared once more as a
tiny white scared-looking West Highland
terrier puppy.

'Wow! That's an amazing disguise!'
Cassie said, completely overwhelmed by
what had just happened. 'Shadow will
never recognize you now.'

Storm blinked up at Cassie with a
troubled expression. 'Shadow will use
his magic to find me as soon as he
can and then no disguise will protect

me. I need to hide now. Can you
help me?'

Cassie's soft heart went out to the
terrified little puppy. With his bright
blue eyes peeking out from behind a
downy fringe, his square little face
and pricked ears, he was the most
adorable thing she had ever seen. 'I'd
really love to. But I don't see how I
can,' she said, chewing her lip. 'We
have to take part in lots of horrible
exercises. I bet some of the families
might think a puppy would slow us
down too much.' Cassie frowned as
she thought about the Ronsons in
particular.

'Do not worry, Cassie!' Storm barked
softly, jumping up and pawing her
waterproof trousers. 'I will use my

magic so that only you can see and
hear me!'

'You mean – you can make yourself
invisible? Cool! Then you can come
with me. Maybe you should do it now
before someone sees you.'

Storm shook himself, so that tiny

sparks flew out of his fluffy white fur. 'It is done.'

'Yay! It's going to be brilliant having someone nice I can talk to this weekend,' Cassie said. 'Wait until I tell Dad about you. He's great at keeping secrets!'

'No! Only you must know I am here. You can never tell anyone. Promise me, Cassie,' Storm woofed, his little face serious.

Cassie felt disappointed that she couldn't even tell her dad the exciting news. But Storm looked so scared, gazing up at her with pleading blue eyes. Cassie decided then and there that if it would help to keep Storm safe, she was prepared to agree.

'OK. Cross my heart and chips don't

fly! That's my own way of saying I promise,' she said as Storm's furry white brow wrinkled in a puzzled frown.

'I've been looking everywhere for you!' an irritated voice suddenly demanded from behind her.

Cassie froze as she recognized Erin's bossy tone.

'Who on earth are you talking to?'

Chapter
THREE

Cassie whipped round guiltily. 'Me? I was just talking to . . . er . . . myself,' she said hastily.

'Your dad sent me to find you,' Erin grumbled. 'I thought you said that you'd be in the girls' loos.'

'Um . . . yeah. I've just . . . er . . . finished in there,' Cassie said distractedly. 'I forgot the way back.'

Storm was sitting there large as life barely a metre away. Even though Storm had said he was now invisible, Cassie couldn't quite believe it. She tensed, waiting for Erin to notice the little puppy. But the older girl didn't comment and Cassie began to relax.

'I'm coming now,' she said, reaching for her rucksack.

'About time too,' Erin scolded.

Storm was now rolling on his back
in the grass. He looked as cute as could
be with his fat pale tummy showing
and all four of his short white legs in
the air. Cassie had to try really hard
not to giggle.

'What's so funny?' Erin asked crossly.

'Nothing,' she said, forcing herself to
concentrate. Luckily, Storm stood up
and shook himself just as an extra big
giggle rose up in her chest. Cassie
hastily turned it into a cough. 'Sorry . . .
er . . . frog in my throat. I bet it's going
to take ages to make a fire and build a
shelter and stuff,' she said, quickly
changing the subject.

Erin smirked. 'Not with *my* dad
helping, it won't! Mum says he's a

whizz with power tools. He can make anything. He made me a brilliant tree house, with a ladder and slide and everything.'

I'd like to see him try to plug in an electric screwdriver in the middle of the forest, Cassie thought, fed up with Erin's boasting.

'Hey!' Erin cried, spotting the chocolate bar on the ground. She swooped down and picked it up. 'Is that yours? You've been having a secret scoff, haven't you?'

'No, I have not!' Cassie said truthfully. Well, it was true that she hadn't eaten any chocolate – yet. And after finding Storm, she'd forgotten all about it. 'Anyway, so what? It's only one measly little bar.'

'It's against the rules to bring your own food. Let's see what the others have to say when I show them this!' Erin waved the bar in the air triumphantly.

'Give it back!' Cassie cried, jumping up to try and reach it, but Erin kept dodging out of her way.

Suddenly, Storm streaked upwards, shedding a glittering rocket's trail of gold sparkles behind him. He shot between Cassie and Erin, grasping the bar in his sharp little teeth. Tossing his head, he pulled the chocolate out of Erin's hand.

'What —' Erin looked up in surprise at her empty hand.

Storm drifted to the ground in another flurry of sparks. Laying back his ears, he bounded away into the bushes.

Cassie bit back another grin. Because Erin couldn't see Storm, she must have thought the chocolate had made a bid to escape by leaping into the air all by itself!

'I don't get it. Where's that chocolate gone?' Erin said, frowning.

'Beats me,' Cassie said casually. She didn't even mind losing the chocolate bar. It was worth it to see the look on Erin's snooty face! Cassie slung her rucksack over her shoulder. 'What are you waiting for? I thought we were in a hurry.'

Still looking puzzled, Erin began following Cassie.

Storm exploded out of the bushes in a flurry of leaves and came tearing over to Cassie with a wide cheeky grin on his little square white face.

'Thanks, Storm. You were brilliant. I don't think Erin will bother snitching on me now that the evidence has gone!' she whispered.

'I am glad I was able to help,' Storm woofed. He stretched and then kicked at the ground with his short back legs, sending a tiny spray of muddy grass in Erin's direction.

Erin skirted sideways to avoid getting spattered. 'There are some mega-freaky breezes in this forest,' she commented.

Cassie thought she was going to burst with laughter. Clapping both hands over her mouth, she broke into a jog. Having Storm as her own special team-mate this weekend was going to be the best fun ever.

Chapter
FOUR

Cassie's spirits were high as the group trekked along a forest track. Storm was gambolling along beside her. Her earlier annoyance at Erin's unfriendliness faded into the background as she thought about her brilliant new puppy friend. The morning flew by and it seemed like about five minutes before they all reached a clearing.

Storm's ears twitched as he looked up at the tall sweet chestnut trees that ringed the area. There were lots of fallen branches, and a thick layer of gold and orange leaves covered everything.

'This is a safe place,' he woofed.

Cassie quickly checked that no one was listening before answering. 'I'm glad you like it. Because it looks like we're

about to set up camp here,' she
whispered.

The instructors explained that the
Reds, Blues and Greens would need to
make everything they needed from
materials they could find around them.
There would also be a special task for
the kids from each team.

'I wonder what that's going to be,'
Cassie whispered to Storm.

He sat at Cassie's feet, all attention.
His fluffy white bottom was parked on
her walking boots. She had to stop
herself from bending down to stroke
him.

'This suddenly seems like an awful lot
of hard work,' her dad said. 'I hope we
haven't actually got to hunt for our
food as well.' His face was red and

sweating from the walk. Cassie could see there were damp patches on his T-shirt through his open shirt.

She gave him a little dig. 'Think of it as a challenge, Dad! The Red team rules, OK!'

He screwed up his face, but then reached across to ruffle her mop of fair curls. 'Well, I'm glad to see that you've perked up. I thought our most difficult task was going to be cheer-up-the-grumpy-daughter!' he teased.

'Da-ad! I wasn't that bad. Was I, Mum?' Cassie said, grinning.

Mrs Yorke smiled and held up her open hands. 'I'm saying nothing!'

Everyone had a drink of bottled water before they started work. Cassie took a swig of hers and then bent down and pretended to be fiddling with her boots. Making sure that no one was watching, she poured some water into her hand for Storm.

His soft whiskery little muzzle tickled her as he lapped it up. 'Thank you, Cassie,' he woofed, licking his chops.

'There'll be a prize for the team who constructs the best shelter and another for the one that gets a fire started first. You might find it helpful to elect a leader,' an instructor was explaining.

Cassie's attention was still on Storm when Mr Ronson's loud voice suddenly made her jump.

'I'll be the Red team's leader,' he boomed. 'I'm the most experienced at outdoor skills. Any objections?' he asked.

'Er . . . well . . .' Mr Yorke murmured,
looking a bit stunned.

'No? That's settled then,' Mr Ronson
said.

After the Blue and Green teams had
decided on their leaders, an instructor
explained about the kids' task. 'While
the adults build a shelter to sleep in,
you're going to look for a hidden

parcel, containing fire-making tools.
There's one for each team. And there'll
be a prize for the team who gets their
fire going first.'

'That sounds like fun,' Cassie
whispered to Storm. 'And you'll be able
to have a good runabout in the forest.'

Storm nodded and eagerly wagged his
stumpy tail.

As the teams moved apart and then
set to work, Mr Ronson took charge.
'Right. You two can start by collecting
some branches. We need to trim them
before we use them to build the shelter,'
he said, jabbing a finger at Cassie's
mum and dad, before turning to his
wife. 'And you can collect some twigs
for firewood. OK, guys, get to it!' he
ordered.

Cassie's dad pulled a wry face at her before he set off towards some fallen branches.

'I see what dad means about Mr Ronson. He's really enjoying bossing everyone about, isn't he? No wonder Erin's so unbearable,' Cassie said to Storm.

Storm growled very softly in agreement.

Cassie suddenly noticed that Erin was looking at her with narrowed eyes and angry flushed cheeks. She realized that she must have spoken more loudly than she'd intended to and Erin had heard her.

She chewed at her lip, feeling guilty. No one liked to hear someone else criticizing their dad. 'Erin, I'm really —'

Cassie was about to apologize, but just then Mr Ronson came over.

'Right, you two. You need to find that hidden package and get back here with it pronto. That prize for lighting a fire first is ours, or I'll want to know the reason why! OK?'

'No problem. I won't let you down, Dad,' Erin said.

'Don't you mean *we* won't let the *team* down?' Cassie asked.

Erin ignored her. 'Does Cassie have to come with me? She'll only lag behind and slow me up!'

Cassie saw Storm's fuzzy white fringe dip in a frown. 'That is not a very kind thing to say!' he yapped.

Cassie agreed with him. 'But I wasn't very nice about her dad, though, was I?

44

Erin's probably just getting her own back on me,' she whispered to him.

But Storm snorted and didn't seem so sure.

'The task is for both of you. Those are the rules, Erin,' Mr Ronson said. He handed Erin a small map and a piece of chalk. 'Why don't you show Cassie how it's done by setting her a good example?'

'If I have to,' Erin said reluctantly, slanting a sideways look at Cassie. 'But it won't be my fault if she messes up.'

Mr Ronson patted his daughter's arm. He smiled down at Cassie. 'I'm sure you'll do your best, dear. A team's only as strong as its weakest member, you know.'

'Charming,' Cassie fumed quietly, but wisely chose not to say anything.

Erin began studying the map as her
dad walked back to the rest of the Reds.

'Can I have a look?' Cassie asked,
going towards her and peering over her
shoulder.

After they had both worked out the

way to go, Erin crumpled up the map and chucked it on the floor.

'Erin!' Cassie cried, indignant at the older girl's littering. But before she could go and pick the map up, she saw Erin already stomping off through the trees.

'Well, come on then,' Erin called back impatiently.

Cassie sighed and she and Storm set off after her. She decided she would pick the map up on their way back.

At first Erin walked at a normal speed, swinging her arms, but the moment they had left the campsite she broke into a run, tearing away from Cassie and Storm.

'Hey! Hang on!' Cassie called to her, speeding up.

Erin looked over her shoulder and waggled her fingers in a wave. 'Come on then, slowcoach!'

Cassie gritted her teeth in determination and broke into a run. She pumped her arms and legs like pistons as she tried to catch up with long-legged Erin. But it was no use. Erin easily out-paced her and was soon out of sight.

Cassie slowed down and then stopped in frustration. 'Oh fudge! Whopping great slurpy slabs of it. I've always been rubbish at running,' she puffed. 'Erin's just going to get the package by herself and then crow about it to everyone. Maybe she was right about me being useless. I should have stayed behind at the camp.'

'That is not true, Cassie. I will help you to catch her up,' Storm woofed.

Suddenly, Cassie felt a strange tingling sensation flowing down her back as bright gold sparks began igniting in Storm's fluffy white fur, and his pointed white ears crackled with electricity.

Something very strange was about to happen!

Chapter
FIVE

Cassie watched in amazement as Storm
lifted one little white paw and sent a
fountain of gold sparks whooshing
towards her. They swirled around,
whirling faster and faster and then
began forming into the shape of a
magnificent horse with a dazzling white
coat and a flowing gold mane and tail.

The next instant, Cassie found herself

seated on the back of the beautiful horse. 'Wow!' she breathed, patting its warm silky neck. 'This is brilliant!'

Storm leapt up in front of her in another little flurry of sparks and Cassie wrapped her hands in the thick golden mane and held on tight. The horse snorted and pawed the ground with one elegant hoof, before it galloped away in a blur of speed. Storm's fluffy white fur rippled in the breeze as they raced along, searching for Erin.

Cassie laughed with delight as trees flashed past them. Now and then the horse veered expertly to one side to avoid a particularly big tree, or weaved through the tall bracken.

'I feel just like Jilly Atkins in *Outback Trail*,' she told Storm.

'Is Jilly one of your friends?' Storm
barked.

'No. She's not a real person. She's a
character in books and computer
games. But I like her because she's
strong and brave and she always tries
to do her best.'

Storm turned to look up at her. 'Just
like you!'

Cassie smiled at him. No one had
ever called her strong and brave
before. 'Look, there's Erin!' she cried,
pointing at a slim figure standing
beneath a spreading oak tree. 'Well
done, Storm!'

Once again, Cassie felt a prickling
sensation down her spine. There was a
flash of golden sparkles. The horse
melted into a wisp of white and gold
smoke before disappearing with a soft
Pop! and then she and Storm were
standing on the leaf-covered ground
behind a thick bush.

Cassie started hurrying towards Erin,
with Storm trotting invisibly beside her.
She pretended to be out of breath as if
she'd been running hard.

Erin turned round as Cassie came

lumbering up to her. 'Oh, it's you,' she
said, scowling.

'Thanks very much for waiting for
me,' Cassie said sarcastically.

'Well, you should have got a move
on. I can't help it if you're a slowcoach,'
Erin scoffed.

Cassie felt her temper rise as Erin hit
a raw nerve. 'Don't call me that!' she
exclaimed in frustration. 'It was your
fault I couldn't keep up. You deliberately
ran off and left me!'

'OK. Keep your hair on,' Erin said
warily, taking a step back. 'Maybe I was
a bit too keen to get going. Anyway,
you're here now, aren't you? Look.
That's where the package must be
hidden.' She pointed up into the
branches where a red flag was fluttering

from a fork in the trunk. 'One of us has
to climb up and get it.'

Cassie could see that the flag was
fairly high up, but the trunk had plenty
of knobbly bits for safe hand and
footholds. She paused, expecting Erin to

leap forward and scale the tree in her usual 'me-first' way.

But Erin looked unusually tense. 'Go on then. What are you waiting for? Climb up there, Cassie!'

But Cassie was fed up with being bossed about. 'Why don't we toss for it? Loser climbs up.' She took a ten-pence piece out of her pocket, tossed it and covered the coin with her hand. 'Your call.'

'Heads!' Erin said.

Cassie uncovered the coin. 'It's tails. You lose.'

'How about best of three?' Erin said promptly.

Cassie shrugged. She tossed the coin twice more and won each time. 'Congratulations! You go up the tree.'

The colour drained from Erin's face. She hung her head. 'I . . . er . . . can't,' she murmured.

Cassie frowned. 'Why not? It's a dead easy climb.'

'I don't like heights, OK?' Erin snapped. 'I suppose you think I'm pathetic now, don't you?'

Cassie was shocked. The way Erin had behaved so far, she didn't think the older girl would be afraid of anything. She was tempted to tease Erin now and get her own back, but seeing how nervous Erin looked she decided not to.

'No, I don't think you're pathetic,' Cassie replied. 'It's no big deal. Everyone's scared of something. I'm not that keen on big hairy spiders.'

Erin looked relieved. 'You won't tell

anyone, will you? Dad doesn't believe in being scared of things. He says everyone has to face their fears. That's what he always does.'

'Yeah, well not everybody's that strong,' Cassie said. 'Of course I won't say anything.'

'Thanks,' Erin said, smiling with genuine warmth for the first time since Cassie had met her. She looked much softer and prettier without the scowl she wore so often.

Cassie found herself wondering for the first time whether she and Erin could become friends. It would be really nice as their dads worked together and they'd probably get to meet each other again in the future.

Cassie took a firm handhold on the

oak's trunk and then braced her foot against a ridge of bark. She swung herself up, climbed up to the fork and reached for the package.

From her high vantage point, she smiled as she caught a glimpse of a small white shape diving into some bracken. Storm was obviously chasing a poor rabbit again!

Cassie climbed down carefully. She had barely reached the ground before Erin grabbed the package out of her hands and tore it open. A small key-ring-like object, but with only two small metal tags, fell into her hands.

'The flint and striker. Now we can go back and get a fire started,' Erin said triumphantly. 'I really want to win that prize. Let's go!'

Cassie followed as Erin set off
confidently. But they had only been
walking for a couple of minutes when
Erin stopped and looked around. 'I'm
not sure which way to go now.'

'Me neither. I can't see any chalk
marks on the trees –' Cassie stopped as
she saw the look on Erin's face.

'I forgot to make any,' Erin
murmured, looking a bit shame-faced.

And Cassie knew why. Erin had been
too intent on leaving her behind to
mark a chalk trail back to camp.

Erin's face fell. 'We're completely lost.
What are we going to do?'

Chapter
SIX

Cassie knew that Storm would easily be able to follow their scent trail back to camp, but he was busy chasing rabbits. With Erin so close, Cassie couldn't call him. She knew that Storm was bound to come and find her soon, but of course she couldn't tell Erin that.

Cassie tried to think of some way of causing a delay. As she shifted her rucksack, she heard a faint crackling of crisp wrappers.

'I think I'll have a quick snack before we start off again,' she said, playing for time. She sat down and took out a bag of crisps. 'Do you want some?'

Erin looked at her in disbelief. 'No, I don't! Don't you care that we're lost?

How can you just sit there stuffing your face?'

'Dead easily,' Cassie said, munching happily. 'Chill out, Erin. Something will turn up; it always does.'

Erin stamped her feet. 'We're going to be *so* late back. I know my dad's counting on winning both prizes. He'll be furious that he can't start the fire.'

'I thought you said he was an expert at outdoor stuff. Can't he rub two sticks together or something?' Cassie suggested reasonably.

'Don't be stupid. That would take ages!' Erin snapped. 'Right! I'm going to try and find my way back now. You can stay here if you like. See if I care.'

'Will you just hang on for thirty seconds? I'm thinking,' Cassie said.

'Yeah, I can hear the rusty wheels going round,' Erin sneered.

'Ha, ha,' Cassie said, thinking that Erin's new friendliness hadn't lasted very long.

Just then, Storm emerged from some tall bracken. He came dashing over with his tongue lolling out and jumped into Cassie's lap. Bits of twig and leaves speckled his white fur. 'I had a very good time. Are we ready to go back now?' he panted.

Cassie pretended to be doing up her rucksack, so that she could whisper to him. 'Yes, but Erin didn't put chalk marks on the trees, so we don't know which way to go. Can you find the way for us, please?'

Storm jumped on to the ground, his

stumpy tail wagging. 'I will be glad to do that!'

'Great.' Cassie jumped to her feet and dusted herself off. 'I think those crisps must have fed my brain because I can remember the way back now,' she said, winking at Storm. 'Follow me, Erin!'

Erin shook her head slowly as Cassie

stomped off. 'You are so annoying, Cassie Yorke!' she cried.

'That makes two of us then,' Cassie said cheerfully.

As Cassie, Storm and Erin walked back into camp, they saw that all three teams were finishing their lean-to shelters. The Blues and Greens had fires blazing in front of theirs.

Cassie's mum called to her as she approached. 'Everything all right, love?'

'Fine. We found the package,' Cassie replied, smiling.

'Well done,' her mum said warmly.

Mr Ronson frowned at Erin. 'All the other kids got back ages ago. What happened? I expected better from you, Erin.'

Erin hung her head. 'I'm sorry . . . I didn't . . .' she began hesitantly.

Cassie felt sorry for her. It couldn't be much fun having such a strict dad. 'It was my fault. I forgot to put any chalk marks on the trees, so we got lost,' she interrupted quickly. 'Erin was great though. We were wandering about for ages, but she somehow found the way back here.'

Mrs Ronson put her arm round her daughter. 'Did you? Well done, Erin.'

Erin threw Cassie a grateful look and gave her a rather shaky smile as she handed the flint and striker to her dad. 'Well, at least we can get the fire started now. Better late than never, I suppose,' Mr Ronson sighed.

'That was a good thing to do. You

are a kind human, Cassie,' Storm
woofed.

'Thanks, Storm. But I think even
Erin deserves to be rescued from such a
bossy dad!' she whispered to him,
smiling.

Cassie and Storm went to see how
their lean-to was coming along. It had
a square frame made of branches lashed
together. More branches leaning against
it formed a slanting open-fronted
shelter. Inside it, a thick layer of
dried leaves made a soft surface for
sleeping on.

'It looks quite cosy in there now,
doesn't it?' Cassie said.

Storm seemed to agree. He
immediately bounded into the shelter
and began nosing around. Leaves flew

in all directions as he scuffed them up
with his front paws.

'Careful. Someone might notice all
this stuff being stirred up by itself,'
Cassie gently reminded him.

Storm put his head on one side,
grinning apologetically. 'I am sorry,
Cassie. There are so many interesting
smells here. I am enjoying exploring
and rooting into everything.'

'Well, that's what puppies do, don't
they?' Cassie said fondly.

Storm nodded happily and suddenly
dashed off towards an interesting-looking
tree stump.

Cassie hid a grin as she watched him.
She felt a surge of affection for her cute
mischievous friend.

Later, Cassie secretly shared her meal

222

of tinned beans and sausages with him. The light began to fade as they were clearing away and the moon rose over the trees. An owl hooted as Cassie was spreading out her sleeping bag.

Erin came over to put hers next to Cassie. 'Thanks for what you said to my dad about it being your fault that we got lost,' she said quietly as they both got ready for bed.

'That's OK,' Cassie said, pleasantly surprised. 'Goodnight, Erin.'

'G'night, Cassie. Sweet dreams,' Erin said sleepily.

Cassie snuggled down with Storm's little warm body next to her. The air was soon filled with soft snores, but she lay awake, enjoying looking out of the open-fronted shelter. The sky was deep purple and blazing with silver stars, like a million tiny diamonds. She wondered whether Storm could see the same stars in his own world.

Cassie felt a deep glow of happiness. 'I love having you here. I hope that you can stay with me forever,' she whispered to him.

Storm twisted his head to look at her, his midnight-blue eyes glowing brightly in the moonlight. 'That is not possible.

One day I must go back to my home world to face Shadow and lead the Moon-claw pack. Do you understand that, Cassie?' he woofed, his little square white face serious.

Cassie nodded sadly but she didn't want to think about that now. This moment was just perfect as it was. She kissed the top of Storm's fluffy white head. 'Sweet dreams,' she yawned as she drifted into sleep.

Chapter
SEVEN

It was cold and misty when Cassie woke the following morning. No one else was awake. She lay snuggled up inside her sleeping bag for a while longer, cuddling Storm's warm stocky little body.

'This is nice and cosy, isn't it?' she whispered, stroking his fluffy fur.

Storm looked up at her and she saw

his midnight-blue eyes darken with
sadness. 'Yes. It is like being curled up
in a safe den with . . . with . . .' he
woofed and then tailed off into a
deep sigh.

*He's thinking of his mother and the
Moon-claw pack in his own world,* Cassie
realized with a pang.

There must be something she could

do to help him feel better. 'I know! How about an early morning walk?' she suggested.

Storm pricked his ears, and his face brightened a little. 'I would like that!' He sprang out of the sleeping bag and wagged his stumpy white tail.

The others were starting to wake up now. So Cassie quickly dressed and pulled on her boots. 'I'll fetch some water for washing,' she called, picking up a bucket.

As she and Storm went off in the direction of the nearby stream, hazy bars of sunlight pushed through the mist hanging over the trees. There was a smoky smell of frosty autumn leaves in the air.

Storm tore around as usual, scrabbling

under fallen logs and sniffing at clumps of grass. He ran towards Cassie with a broken branch in his mouth and dropped it at her feet. Crouching down on to his front paws, he barked hopefully.

Cassie laughed and threw the branch for him to fetch. With a happy bark, Storm ran after it. He seemed to be feeling much happier than when he woke up – just as Cassie hoped he would.

She swung her arms as she walked, feeling perfectly happy. At the stream, she kneeled down to fill the bucket from a spring gushing down over some rocks. Storm was splashing about in the shallows a few metres away.

He jumped out on to the bank and came lolloping up to Cassie. His white

fur stuck up in little wet peaks and
there was a cheeky expression on his
dripping face.

'Don't you dare –' Cassie began, but
it was too late.

Storm's whole body shivered from
head to foot as he shook himself. A
shower of droplets splashed all over
Cassie.

'Storm! You little terror! You did that on purpose!' she scolded laughingly. 'It's a good thing I'm wearing waterproofs.'

Storm beamed and stood up on his short back legs to paw at her trousers. His sharp puppy teeth were very white against his little black lips.

As they made their way back to camp, the delicious smell of frying bacon floated towards them.

'I like human food,' Storm yapped hungrily.

Cassie's mouth watered too. Why did food always smell so much better outdoors?

'Hello, love. You're an early bird this morning,' Mrs Yorke said as she turned rashers in the pan.

Mr Yorke was just opening a tin of tomatoes.

'Hiya, parents,' Cassie sang out as she put down the bucket of water. Storm's cheerfulness was infectious. 'I was wide awake, so I thought I'd do something useful.'

Her dad goggled his eyes. 'Quick, someone, call the police! Someone's stolen our Cassie and swapped her for this helpful, strangely cheerful girl!' he joked.

'Da-ad!' Cassie pretended to swipe him on the head.

She wished she could tell them that the reason why she was so happy was sitting there invisibly, wagging his little white tail. Cassie would have loved to see the look on their faces, but she

knew that she would never give away
Storm's secret.

That afternoon there were team games.
The most fun was when each person
took it in turn to be blindfolded and
then their team-mates talked them
through an obstacle course.

'I will make myself glow very
brightly and you will be able to see me
through the band round your eyes. You
can just follow me,' Storm woofed,
eager to take part.

'No. That would be cheating. I have
to do this myself, but thanks anyway,'
Cassie told him.

So instead, Storm joined in by
padding around on tiptoe behind the
person wearing the blindfold. Cassie

laughed so much that others began to laugh too and even Erin joined in.

'I didn't think this game was *that* funny!' Erin said, giggling and wiping her eyes.

'It's not!' Cassie spluttered.

Later there was more firewood to collect and then a short talk about identifying and collecting wild food. Time passed quickly for Cassie and soon, after supper, everyone sat round in a circle to do a task together.

'You can make everything you need from the materials around you. We're going to make some cord from a plant you can find growing almost anywhere,' the instructor said, producing a bundle of green stems.

'Ouch! Stinging nettles!' Cassie said nervously.

Storm twitched one ear. After having rushed about all day, he was lying next to her with his nose resting on his paws.

'Hold your nettle like this,' said the instructor, holding the stalks at an angle. 'Now, push firmly upwards to strip off the leaves. Try it. You won't get stung if you do it like this.'

'It would be far easier if we all wore gloves,' Mr Yorke joked.

Cassie grinned at him.

'Gloves?' Mr Ronson scoffed, obviously taking her dad seriously. 'I suppose you'll want a cushion to sit on next! Come on, man. Rise to the challenge!' He pushed up his sweatshirt sleeves, flexed his bulging muscles and then began rubbing his palms together noisily.

As her dad's face reddened, Cassie tingled with embarrassment on his behalf.

She couldn't stand the way Erin's dad always had to show off.

'Me first!' she shouted on impulse. Gritting her teeth she leaned forward and grabbed a big hairy nettle, exactly as the instructor had shown her. It didn't sting at all. She ran her hands upwards towards the top and the leaves fell off on to the grass.

'Da-dah!' Cassie crowed, waving the stripped stem in the air.

Mr Ronson looked at her in surprise. 'Not bad,' he said.

Coming from him, that was praise indeed, Cassie thought.

As everyone got to work stripping nettles, the instructor showed Cassie the next stages in making cord.

Cassie felt a tiny tingle down her spine. Next to her, little gold sparks

were starting to glisten in Storm's
white fur.

She suddenly found herself
smoothing, flattening, rolling and
twisting, her nimble fingers flying. In
half a minute she had her first ever
piece of strong green cord. 'Storm.
I can do this by myself,' she scolded
gently.

Storm nodded. The sparks in his fur
went out. He gave a contented sigh and
began dozing as Cassie carried on
making nettle cord by herself.

'Are you sure you haven't done this
before? You're a natural,' the instructor
said as the pile of cord in front of her
grew.

'I've always loved making things. I
guess it's some consolation for being

rubbish at sports and stuff,' Cassie said modestly.

The instructor smiled. 'A good team needs "doers" and "makers". It's all about sharing skills.'

Cassie hadn't thought of it like that before. She felt a stir of pride. Perhaps being part of a team was something she could be good at after all.

On the other side of the circle, Erin grinned encouragingly.

Chapter
EIGHT

Later that evening, the instructors left for the cabin, intending to return early the following morning.

'You should all be fine by yourselves for a few hours. But we're not far away and we'll leave you a mobile phone in case of emergencies,' one of them said.

'I'll hold on to that phone,' Mr

Ronson said promptly, tucking it into his pocket.

It was another clear night. Trees cast long shadows in the moonlight as the Blues, Greens and Reds prepared for bed.

Cassie settled down with Storm. 'It's Sunday tomorrow. We go home after lunch. You're going to love it there,' she told him.

Storm gave a tiny woof and yawned sleepily. He turned round and round in

circles before settling comfortably with his head resting beneath Cassie's chin.

Cassie said her goodnights to everyone and instantly fell asleep.

She woke suddenly a few hours later, in the dark-grey light of dawn. There was a loud drumming noise all around her. At first Cassie couldn't understand what the noise was and then a cold raindrop splashed on to her nose.

She crawled to the open front of the shelter and peered out. Rain was coming down in torrents through the trees. In the semi-darkness, she could just see wriggly lines of water trickling past the shelter. A huge puddle glistened across what had been grass the night before and reached almost to the Greens' tent.

Storm stood up and shook himself.
Lifting his nose, he sniffed the air.
'There is too much water. We could be
in danger,' he yapped, flattening his ears.

'You mean floods? I'd better wake
everyone up!' Cassie leapt up and
scrambled into her clothes. She leaned
over to shake Erin, who was nearest,
and then woke both sets of parents.
'Quick! There's water everywhere!' she
told them.

'It's just a bit of rain, for goodness'
sake.' Mr Ronson's voice was muffled
from deep within his sleeping bag. 'Stop
fussing and go back to sleep.'

Storm lifted his lip in a soft growl
and danced sideways, barking in
annoyance. Cassie felt like doing the
same thing.

'No! We have to move. Storm says so!' she burst out, hardly realizing what she'd said. Luckily, no one seemed to have heard her properly.

'What's that about a storm, Cass?' her dad asked sleepily, opening one eye. His hair was all sticking up. 'Are you sure you didn't just have a bad dream?'

'I'm not imagining this. Please, Dad, just take a look outside,' Cassie said desperately.

'OK. Anything for a bit of peace,' Mr Yorke groaned.

Suddenly, Erin cried out. 'There's water coming in. Ugh! My sleeping bag's getting soaked!'

Mr Yorke sat bolt upright. 'Crikey! Cassie's right. If we don't move soon, we'll be sitting in the middle of a lake!

Look, the Greens and Blues are already getting up!'

After that, there was a mad scramble to get dressed into waterproofs and roll up the sleeping bags. Cassie picked Storm up and cradled him in her arms, keeping him dry beneath her baggy anorak.

As they all splashed across to join up with the other families, the instructors' mobile phone rang. Mr Ronson answered it.

Cassie and Erin were closest to him and both heard some of what he said. 'No, there's no need for you to do that. It's not that bad here. Yes, I'm absolutely certain. We can make it back by ourselves,' Mr Ronson said confidently. 'OK. I'll explain to the others. No probs. Leave it to me.'

Cassie frowned in puzzlement. Something didn't seem quite right about the conversation. 'I wonder what's going on. What isn't there any need for the instructors to do?' she whispered to Storm.

Mr Ronson began speaking. 'We've been told to make our way back to the cabin. There's a short cut across a bridge, just over that ridge. I went and checked it out yesterday afternoon,' he explained.

'That seems a roundabout way to go, when we could go via the track we came in on,' Mr Yorke commented.

Mr Ronson shrugged. 'That's as may be. But this is the *Wild Wood Experiences* way and the sooner we get moving, the sooner we'll be back. Hurry up now; this way, everyone,' he said, waving one arm in a big arc.

'He'll be shouting "Wagons roll!" in a minute, like in those awful old cowboy films!' Cassie grumbled.

Her dad laughed. 'Remind me to buy him a sheriff's badge sometime.'

Cassie tramped along, feeling happy that they were all safe, despite the rain dripping from her anorak hood. Storm's little body was warm against her chest and she could smell his faint clean puppy scent. 'Are you OK in there?' she whispered, looking down at him.

Storm reached up and licked her chin. 'I am fine.'

The rain slowed and then stopped as they trudged along. After about ten minutes, they reached the top of the ridge. The ground sloped steeply downwards on the other side. At the bottom, Cassie could see the ditch with the wooden footbridge over it.

Suddenly, she heard fierce growling and barking through the trees. Cassie felt Storm stiffen and begin to tremble all over. 'What's wrong?' she asked softly.

'I think Shadow is close. He will have used his magic to make any dogs that are nearby into my enemies. Now he has set them on to me,' Storm whimpered softly, rolling his eyes in terror.

'Those dogs do sound like they're getting closer,' Cassie said worriedly. 'How will I be able to tell if they're coming for you?'

Storm whimpered and Cassie could feel his heart beating wildly. 'They will have fierce pale eyes and extra-long teeth.'

The sound of growling was even louder. Cassie felt a leap of fear. Storm was in terrible danger! She racked her brains as she tried to think of some way of protecting the tiny puppy.

A memory stirred within her. In one of her favourite books, Jilly Atkins had been tracked by a hungry bear and had escaped by rubbing something very nasty indeed all over herself to disguise her scent.

'That's it!' Cassie burst out. Without a second thought, she pretended to lose her balance and slip over. 'Oh,' she cried as she skidded for real and both legs shot from beneath her.

She landed on her backside with a teeth-rattling jolt. Gathering speed, Cassie went sliding downwards in a slippery muddy avalanche of half-rotten leaves.

Chapter
NINE

Taking care to cradle Storm in both hands, Cassie twisted sideways and began rolling over and over down the slope. She wanted to make certain that she was covered in smelly stuff from head to foot.

As Cassie tumbled to the bottom, she found herself heading towards a big clump of brambles, but couldn't put out her hands to stop herself. Sharp thorns tore at her clothes and made deep scratches in her skin, but Cassie hardly noticed them.

Tearing herself free, she scrambled to her feet. A strong earthy pong rose up around her.

'Perfect! No enemy dogs will be able

to smell you through this stuff,' Cassie said.

'Thank you, Cassie,' Storm whined softly. 'That was very brave. You could have been badly hurt.'

'I couldn't bear anything to happen to you,' Cassie said. 'Oh,' she gasped, as the scratches started throbbing now that the excitement was over.

'You *are* hurt! I will make you better,' Storm yapped.

Cassie felt a familiar prickling down her spine as Storm huffed out a glittery puppy breath. The softly gleaming cloud floated into the air and then sprinkled down on to Cassie like Christmas glitter. As the golden dust dissolved into her muddy clothes, she felt the soreness fading and all the rips and tears mended themselves instantly.

'Thanks, Storm,' she said, stroking his little warm ears. 'I think you'd better stay inside my anorak until we're completely certain that those fierce dogs have gone.'

The fear was starting to fade from Storm's deep blue eyes, but he nodded. 'I think so too.'

'Cassie!' her mum shouted in a panicky voice, hurtling down the slope ahead of the others. 'Are you hurt?'

'No. I'm just a bit shaken up,' Cassie replied.

'Thank goodness for that. I can't believe you've escaped without even a scratch or the tiniest rip in your clothes. You're a very lucky girl!'

'I know,' Cassie said. *I'm the luckiest*

girl in the whole world — I've got Storm for a friend, she thought.

Cassie's mum wrinkled her nose. 'But just look at the state of you! Phew! You smell dreadful!'

'I don't mind,' Cassie said happily.

'You're going to need a shower when we get back to the cabin,' her dad said on reaching her. 'You clumsy old sausage. Fancy falling down that

slope. It's the sort of thing I usually do!' he said.

Cassie realized that he was about to give her a comforting hug, despite the smelly mud. 'No, don't, Dad! You'll get all stinky too,' she said quickly, backing away. If he squeezed her, he'd be sure to feel Storm's sturdy little body beneath her anorak.

Mr Ronson came stamping over. 'For goodness' sake! Can't that girl do anything right? Of all the useless –'

'Don't, Dad! Cassie's OK,' Erin cried from just behind him. 'And it's not her fault anyway. We didn't have to come this way, did we?'

Cassie's jaw dropped in astonishment. Did Erin just stick up for her?

'What does Erin mean?' asked Mr Yorke.

Mr Ronson looked rather uncomfortable as the others gazed at him enquiringly.

A light seemed to go on in Cassie's head as she remembered the mobile-phone conversation. It was starting to make sense now. 'You weren't told to bring us back this way, were you? That was all your own idea!'

'Is this true, Ronson?' asked one of the other dads.

Mr Ronson nodded slowly. 'They were going to send a van to pick us up and told us to meet it at the track. But I told them not to bother. We came here for the challenge, didn't we? I thought you'd all welcome the chance of getting back under our own steam.'

'But you didn't bother to ask us if we

agreed with you, did you?' Mr Yorke said angrily. 'As a team member, you're the worst. Not to mention that Cassie could have been badly hurt when she tumbled down that muddy slope!'

'But I'm fine, Dad!' Cassie protested.

'That's not the point.' Her dad squared his shoulders and stood his ground in front of the taller man. 'What do you say, Ronson?'

Mr Ronson shifted his feet. 'OK. I

admit that I was wrong. I'm sorry, everyone.' He turned to Cassie. 'And I'm truly sorry that you almost got hurt. I'll call the cabin right now and tell them to send the van for us after all.'

'You do that!' Mr Yorke said. He looked at Cassie and her mum. 'Let's skirt round this ridge and make our way to the track.'

Everyone else began following as the Yorkes set off. Cassie hung back to thank Erin, but the older girl avoided her eyes and linked arms with her dad.

Cassie sighed as she went to catch up with her mum and dad. 'I thought Erin might feel like walking back together, but she doesn't seem to want anything to do with me,' she whispered disappointedly to Storm.

'Perhaps she just needs more time,' Storm woofed wisely. 'It could not have been easy for her to stand up to her father.'

Cassie nodded. 'That's true.' She hoped that Storm was right about Erin needing more time, but she was starting to think that they would never be friends.

Chapter
TEN

To Cassie's immense relief, there was no more growling or barking as she and Storm made their way to the track, along with the others.

'I think this smelly mud has done the trick. Shadow's dogs must have gone past,' Cassie said.

Storm nodded, his midnight-blue eyes thoughtful. 'Your plan has worked for the moment. But I sense that those dogs are not too far away. If they return, I may have to leave suddenly.'

Cassie felt a pang as she realized that she didn't feel ready ever to let her magical little friend go. She loved being with Storm so much.

'I'm looking forward to getting

warm,' she said, deliberately changing the subject. 'And I want a mega-sized mug of hot chocolate and a mountain of biscuits, so I can share them with you!'

Storm perked up and licked his little chops. 'That sounds good!'

A big minibus was waiting on the track. The group all piled inside. Cassie lifted the bottom of her anorak, so that Storm could crawl out. She sat with him on her lap, stroking his fluffy white fur.

Back at the cabin, everyone began changing into dry clothes. With so many people inside, it was rather cramped. There were wet boots, rucksacks and waterproofs everywhere.

'Come on, young lady. Let's get you

straight into the shower,' said Cassie's
mum. 'Here you are. You can change
into these.' She thrust a bundle of dry
clothes into her arms.

Cassie went into the large washroom.
She soaped and scrubbed herself,
enjoying the hot water. Steam filled the
shower cubicle, so that Cassie didn't
notice Storm press himself into the
corner by the door and then keep
looking round nervously.

After Cassie finished drying herself,
she pulled on her jeans and T-shirt and
dry trainers.

Just as Cassie and Storm came out of
the shower, Cassie almost bumped into
Erin, who was bent over with her head
under a wall-mounted dryer.

'Hi,' Cassie said.

Erin stood up and flicked her damp hair back. 'Hi.'

Cassie chewed her lip, trying to think of something to say. 'I'm . . . er . . .' she began.

'No, let me go first,' Erin said. She took a deep breath and then out it all came in a rush. 'I don't suppose you'd . . . er . . . want to come to my house sometime, would you? I know I've been a brat and my dad can be a bit stern and bossy, but he's OK when you get to know him better. And I've just got this brilliant new computer game with Jilly Atkins in and I thought we could – what?' she asked, as Cassie stood there open-mouthed.

'I can't believe it. You like Jilly Atkins?' Cassie said delightedly.

Erin nodded. 'I absolutely love her. I've read all her books, except the new one.'

'Me too! I'm reading the new one now. You can borrow it after me, if you like,' Cassie said, smiling all over her face.

Erin beamed back at her. 'Cool! So you'll get your dad to bring you over?'

'I'd love to!' Cassie said.

This weekend had turned out really well after all. Cassie had to admit that the team building had worked a treat — at least for her and Erin.

She was still taking these amazing developments in, when Storm suddenly gave a sharp whine of terror and shot towards the washroom door. At that moment, someone came in and Storm bolted straight out of the gap.

Cassie's tummy clenched. Storm's enemies must have come back. He was in terrible danger. Leaping forward, she ran after Storm. 'Back in a minute,' she called to a puzzled-looking Erin.

Cassie pounded down the corridor. Right at the end of it, she saw Storm's stocky little white form dash round a

door with *Storeroom* written on it. From
somewhere just outside, she could hear
loud snarls and growls.

As Cassie reached the storeroom,
a dazzling flash of bright gold light
streamed out of it. Nervous about
what might happen, she slowly
opened the door more widely and
went inside.

There was Storm, a tiny helpless
puppy no longer, but his true majestic
self: a beautiful young silver-grey wolf
with glowing midnight-blue eyes. An
older wolf with a gentle face, whom
Cassie guessed was his mother, stood
next to him.

And then Cassie knew that Storm
was leaving for good. She was going to
have to be very brave. She rushed over

and Storm allowed her to hug him one last time.

'I'll never forget you, Storm,' Cassie said, her voice breaking as she buried her face in his thick soft fur.

'You have been a good friend. I will remember you too,' Storm said in a deep velvety growl.

Cassie took a step back just as an ugly growl sounded right outside the

door. 'Go. Save yourself, Storm!' she urged, her heart aching.

There was a final burst of brilliant gold light and a bright shower of sparks floated down all around Cassie and crackled on the storeroom floor. Storm and his mother faded and then were gone. The growl was abruptly cut off and silence fell.

Cassie felt her throat sting with tears. She was going to miss Storm terribly, but at least she knew he was safe. And she would always have her secret memories of the wonderful adventure they'd shared.

'Cassie? Where are you?' called Erin's voice from the corridor.

'Coming!' Cassie called, making for the door. She took a deep breath and silently wished magic puppy Storm and his Moon-claw pack well as, smiling, she went to find her new friend for some adventures of their own.

If you like
Magic Puppy,
you'll love

Magic Kitten

A Summer Spell
9780141320144

Classroom Chaos
9780141320151

Star Dreams
9780141320168

Double Trouble
9780141320175

Moonlight Mischief
9780141321530

A Circus Wish
9780141321547

Sparkling Steps
9780141321554

A Glittering Gallop
9780141321561

Seaside Mystery
9780141321981

Firelight Friends
9780141321998

A Shimmering Splash
9780141322001

A Puzzle of Paws
9780141322018

A Christmas Surprise
9780141323237

Picture Perfect
9780141323480

A Splash of Forever
9780141323497

Coming Soon

Magic Puppy

A little puppy, a sprinkling of magic, a forever friend.

Twirling Tails   School of Mischief

puffin.co.uk

Magic Puppy

Win a Magic Puppy goody bag!

The evil wolf Shadow has ripped out part of Storm's letter from his mother and hidden the words so that magic puppy Storm can't find them.

Storm needs your help!

Two words have been hidden in secret bones in *A Forest Charm* and *Party Dreams*. Find the hidden words and put them together to complete the message from Storm's mother. Send it in to us and each month we will put every correct message in a draw and pick out one lucky winner, who will receive a Magic Puppy gift – definitely worth barking about!

Send the hidden message, your name and address on a postcard to:
Magic Puppy Competition
Puffin Books
80 Strand
London WC2R 0RL
Good luck!

puffin.co.uk